TONI MORRISON
& SLADE MORRISON

Please,
Louise

Illustrated by
SHADRA
STRICKLAND

A Paula Wiseman Book
SIMON & SCHUSTER
BOOKS FOR YOUNG READERS
New York London Toronto Sydney New Delhi

SIMON & SCHUSTER BOOKS FOR YOUNG READERS
An imprint of Simon & Schuster Children's Publishing Division
1230 Avenue of the Americas, New York, New York 10020

For information about special discounts for bulk purchases,
please contact Simon & Schuster Special Sales at 1-866-506-1949 or business@simonandschuster.com.
The Simon & Schuster Speakers Bureau can bring authors to your live event.
For more information or to book an event, contact the Simon & Schuster Speakers Bureau
at 1-866-248-3049 or visit our website at www.simonspeakers.com.
Book design by Laurent Linn
The text for this book is set in Minister Std.
The illustrations for this book are rendered in watercolor, gouache, pencil, and crayon.
Manufactured in China
1213 SCP
2 4 6 8 10 9 7 5 3 1
Library of Congress Cataloging-in-Publication Data
Morrison, Toni.
Please, Louise / Toni Morrison ; Slade Morrison ; illustrated by Shadra Strickland. — 1st ed.
p. cm.
"A Paula Wiseman Book."
Summary: On a gray, rainy day, everything seems particularly frightening and bad to Louise until she enters a
library and finds books that help her to know and imagine the beauty and wonder that have been there all along.
ISBN 978-1-4169-8338-5 (hardcover : alk. paper) — ISBN 978-1-4424-3310-6 (eBook)
[1. Books and reading—Fiction. 2. Fear—Fiction. 3. Libraries—Fiction.] I. Morrison, Slade.
II. Strickland, Shadra, ill. III. Title.
PZ7.M845147Ple 2013
[E]—dc23
2012026303

first
edition

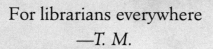
For librarians everywhere
—*T. M.*

For August, Chainey, Hannah, and Jersey Rose, with love
—*S. S.*

Please, Louise, please, please.
Things are not always what they seem.
If you are sometimes lonely or sometimes sad,
know that the world is big but not so bad.

The sky is gray now but not for long.
After the rain, birds break into song.
Please, Louise, please, please.
There's nothing hiding in those trees.

Don't scurry too fast and miss the music of the street.
You may be surprised by who or what you meet.

You frown at the yard where that old car is parked
and shrink from the sound of a little dog's bark.

Is that house really haunted? Or does it just need care?
Why not imagine the joy that used to be there?

Is that a junkyard? Or a dangerous trap,
where ghosts live and monsters nap?
Scary thoughts are your creation
when you have no information.

Sheets of rain, black clouds, thunder.

Hurry! Find a roof to get under!

Is that a bird of prey from which you'd better run?

Or an eagle of gold when touched by the sun?

Here is shelter from any storm.
In this place you are never alone.

These books are loyal friends, helping you explore,
dream, discover, think, learn, and know much, much more.

Imagination is an open door.
Step in here and let it soar.

"Venice is a city that sits in the sea. . . ."

"When pirate ships sailed the ocean lanes . . ."

"Dolphins are the most social . . ."

"The princess sat weeping in her chamber . . . "

"Juju the lion cub was lost.

He could not find his mother."

See, little girl, this is your world.
So smile awhile as the stories unfurl
where beauty and wonder cannot hide.
Because reading books is a pleasing guide.

Fear and sadness—where did they go?
Louise doesn't care. Louise doesn't know.

She can understand what she feels,
since books can teach and please Louise.